Take the Time

Mindfulness for Kids

by Maud Roegiers

MAGINATION PRESS • WASHINGTON, DC

American Psychological Association

Prendre le temps by Maud Roegiers
Copyright © 2009 Alice Éditions
Translated from the French by Julia Frank-McNeil

When everything is topsy-turvy
with my head spinning
and my feet up in the air,

Take the Time
Mindfulness for Kids

Published by
MAGINATION PRESS
An Educational Publishing Foundation Book
American Psychological Association
750 First Street, NE
Washington, DC 20002

Printed by Worzalla, Stevens Point, WI

Library of Congress Cataloging-in-Publication Data

Take the time : mindfulness for kids / by Maud Roegiers ; translated from the French
by Julia Frank-McNeil.
p. cm.
Translation of Prendre le temps
ISBN-13: 978-1-4338-0794-7 (hardcover : alk. paper)
ISBN-10: 1-4338-0794-7 (hardcover : alk. paper)
ISBN-13: 978-1-4338-0796-1 (pbk. : alk. paper)
ISBN-10: 1-4338-0796-3 (pbk. : alk. paper) 1. Self-consciousness (Awareness)—
Juvenile literature. 2. Self-help techniques—Juvenile literature. I. Title.

B105.C477R6413 2010
155.42'3—dc22   2009052915

First printing March 2010

10 9 8 7 6 5 4 3 2

I slow down and take the time

to be with my friends,

To stick to things I know,

To close my eyes when I am hugged,

To let the cold tickle my cheeks,

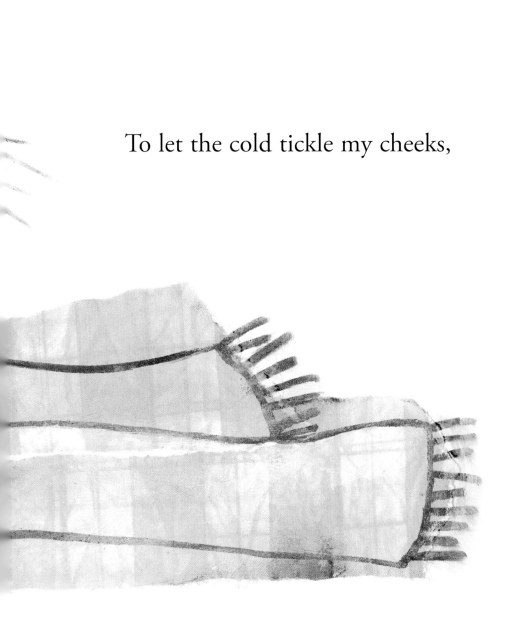

To do things that make me feel good.

I take the time

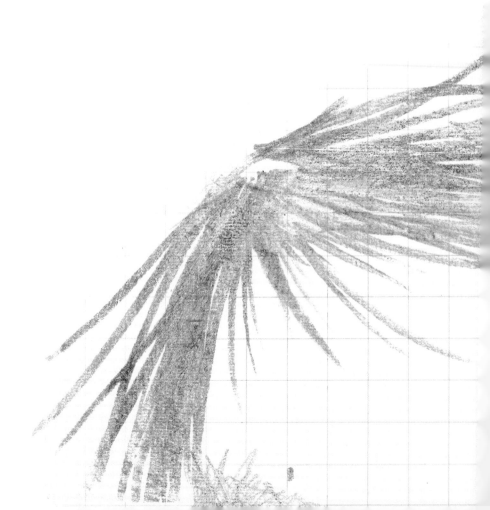

to think about what I am doing,

Before I share a secret,

Before I blurt something out.

I take the time to fix

my little mistakes,

And to be sad, if I need to.

To think about what I've dreamt,

To listen to silence,

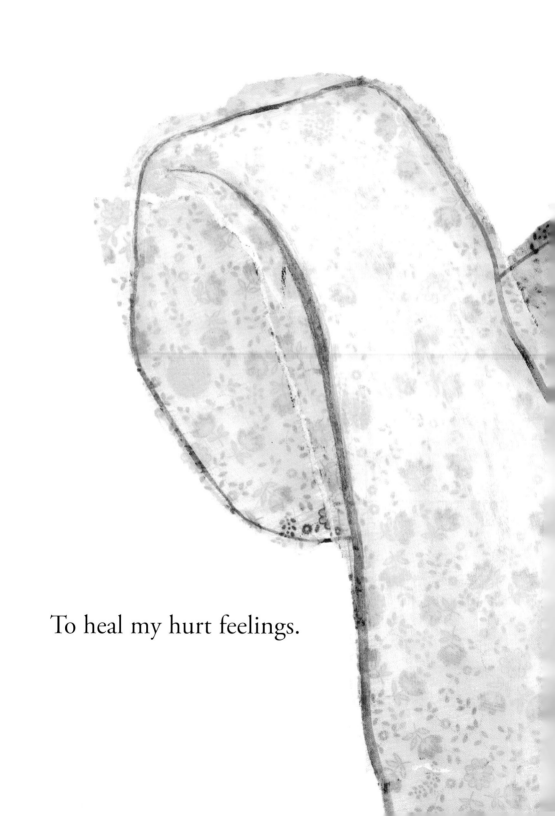

To heal my hurt feelings.

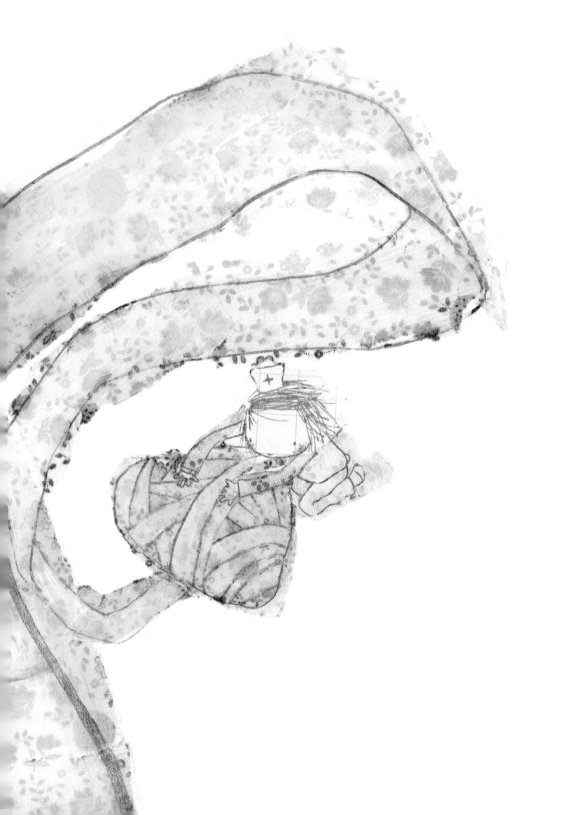

I take the time to love,

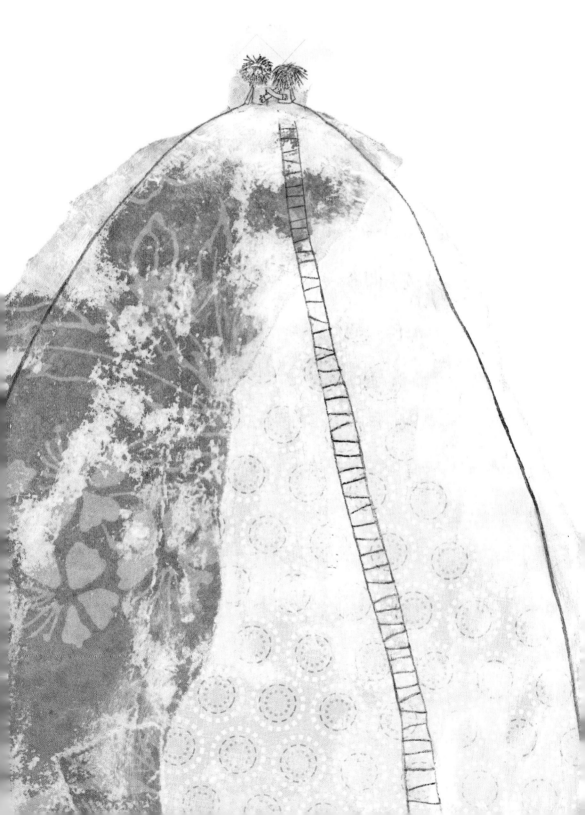

And then I feel better.